DANNY DINGLE'S

FANTASTIC FINDS

Angie Lake

The Jet of Justice

Published by Sweet Cherry Publishing Limited
Unit 36, Vulcan House
Vulcan Road
Leicester, LE5 3EF
United Kingdom

www.sweetcherrypublishing.com

First published in the UK in 2017
ISBN: 978-1-78226-261-9

Danny Dingle's Fantastic Finds: The Jet of Justice

Printed and bound by Thomson Press (India) Limited.

DANNY DINGLE'S

FANTASTIC FINDS

Book 3

The Jet of Justice

Written by Angie Lake
Illustrated by Shanith MM

DANNY DINGLE'S SUPER-SECRET SPY NOTEBOOK.

DO NOT READ (unless you are Danny, Percy or Superdog.)

This book is guarded by **EVIL EDGAR**: an invisible hedgehog with military training.

Continue at your own risk!

You have been **WARNED**. . .

So, Evil Edgar may not have been the best bodyguard.

But you would have been in trouble if you were a SLUG! Or a tin of CAT FOOD!

Anyway. . .

Let me get you up to speed.

This is me, the **WORLD FAMOUS** (almost) **GENIUS** inventor, Danny Dingle.

And this is **Superdog**, my psychic 'pet' toad.

I should probably warn you now that, although he may look like a toad, Superdog is a **GENIUS** in disguise. Honestly, he's so **SUPER-INTELLIGENT** and **CRAFTY** that Mum won't let him in the house anymore.

We live in a house, or **MADHOUSE**, as I like to call it, in Greenville.

I also go to school in Greenville. But I'm not going to talk about school seeing as it's the **SUMMER HOLIDAYS** and I get to spend my days doing super-C**OO**L **GENIUS** things like:

- Reading lots of Metal Face comics

World's Best Superhero EVER!

\- Trying to do the world's **BIGGEST** and most **iMPRESSiVE** fart

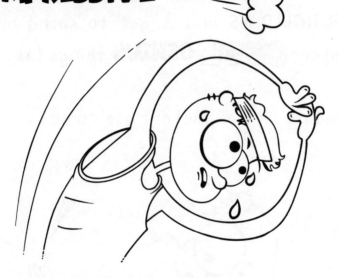

BOOM...

- Go out searching for fantastic finds so I can make my **GENIUS** inventions

COOL STUFF

\-   Hang out with my best friend and slightly 'dopey' assistant, Percy McDuff

\- Hide out in my **SECRET** laboratory (which is cleverly disguised as a normal clubhouse) and create **AMAZING INVENTIONS** with Superdog and Percy

Now, you have to understand that not just anybody can come up with all of these **GENIUS** inventions – they don't just fall out of thin air!

For a start, you need a super-secret, super-special inventor's kit that you MUST carry around with you at all times, the kit should include:

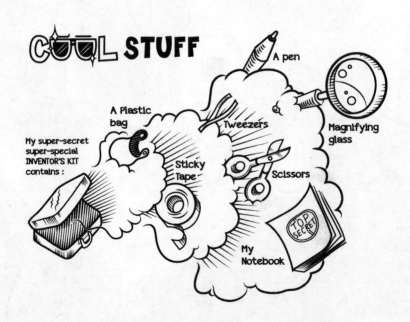

COOL STUFF

A pen

A Plastic bag

Tweezers

Magnifying glass

My super-secret super-special INVENTOR'S KIT contains:

Sticky Tape

Scissors

TOP SECRET

My Notebook

And you must **ALWAYS BE ON THE LOOKOUT!!**

And, of course, you have to be a **GENIUS!!!**

$E = mc^2$

All of my awesome inventions are made from things I find when I'm out and about. These are my fantastic finds, and Percy does a great job of organising them into jars and pots in the **super-secret** lab **CLUBHOUSE**.

So far this summer, Superdog and I have managed to gather **loads** of things, including:

A COAT HANGER

TOP SECRET BLUEPRINTS

SOMEONE'S LOST BUNCH OF KEYS

A SCRATCHED CD

ELASTIC BANDS

A SHOPPING TROLLEY

You see, from all of this **COOL STUFF**, we made a mobile for my baby sister, Mel.

19

We also invented:

THE MIGHTY WALKING WHEEL

As you can see, it's made of an old person's walking stick and the wheel of a supermarket trolley.

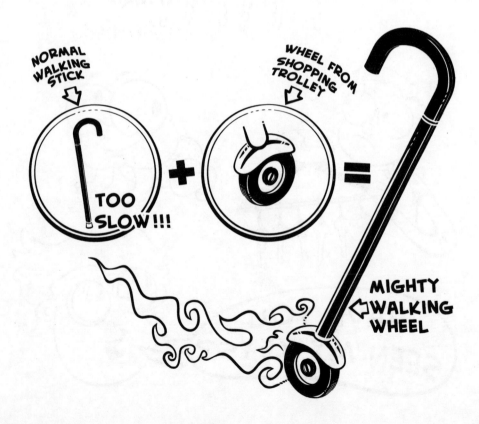

NORMAL WALKING STICK

TOO SLOW!!!

WHEEL FROM SHOPPING TROLLEY

MIGHTY WALKING WHEEL

You may have noticed that people who use walking sticks are SUPER-SLOW... but with the MIGHTY WALKING WHEEL those days are over. The stick just keeps going and going!

LIGHTNING FAST GRANNIES!

So far it's at the experimental stage. We tested it on Mrs Dawkins at number 43.

We exchanged her normal walking stick for the Mighty Walking Wheel without her knowing.

Unfortunately she hadn't been properly trained in its use. She slid straight down the hill and broke her jaw.

OBVIOUSLY, we'll have to include an instruction manual next time.

So after all of this, I think Mum was getting a bit '**SICK**' of us.

She lectured us over tea and made us take Mrs Dawkins a bunch of flowers and apologise.

GET WELL SOON...

I wanted to take Superdog with us, because it was partly his fault too, but Mum didn't let us. She said: "Mrs Dawkins has suffered enough, I don't see how taking that **SMELLY TOAD** round is going to help things."

Mum really doesn't like Superdog, even though he eats all the nasty, SCARY spiders that everyone is afraid of.

(Everyone except me, I'm not afraid of spiders, HONEST!)

Anyway, Percy and I went to apologise to Mrs Dawkins. I took her some flowers. Percy took her a **BiG** tin of toffees.

Mrs Dawkins really liked the flowers, but she looked quite cross about the toffee.

I'D GIVE THESE BOYS A GOOD TELLING OFF IF ONLY I COULD OPEN MY MOUTH AND TALK!

After that, Mum decided that having us hanging around all summer was probably going to be a

'DANGER TO THE WHOLE NEIGHBOURHOOD'.

YOU NEED TO FIND SOMETHING TO OCCUPY YOURSELF INSTEAD OF GETTING INTO TROUBLE! I'M SENDING YOU TO SUMMER CAMP!

NO WAY! I CAN'T GO TO SUMMER CAMP, I HAVE SO MANY TOP-SECRET, I MEAN, BRILLIANT THINGS TO DO HERE!

YOU EITHER GO TO SUMMER CAMP OR I CAN FIND YOU PLENTY OF

CHORES

TO DO.

I haven't always had the most fun at camps, but there was **NO WAY** I was helping Mum for the whole summer.

Mum seems to have forgotten that I need to spend **ALL** of my time making cool super-inventions so I can become genius-inventor-assistant to **METAL FACE**, the world's most awesome and

FARTASTIC superhero!

Summer camp definitely sounded better than what Mum would have got me doing, though:

-    Weeding the garden

Playing with Mel

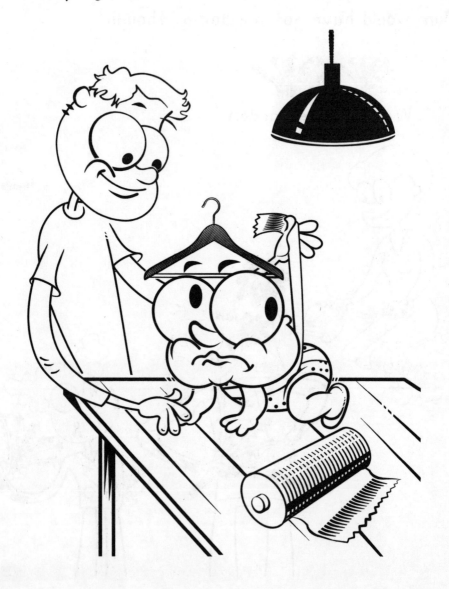

- Putting all the CDs and DVDs in alphabetical order

Dad said this was also good because it would give him time to work on his

He's been working on the recipe for years.

But **unfortunately,** Mum doesn't let him carry out his experiments in the house.

So we decided that whilst we were gone, he could use the clubhouse. Mum thought it was a great idea, she said that:

"Dad's DESTRUCTIVE powers are best kept outdoors"

Dad made us a **huge batch** of his regular fart-jelly to take with us.

So off we went to summer camp!!

Percy and I hoped this one would be better than our last camping experience.

Last time, our tent got washed down the river, we had to peel potatoes **ALL THE TIME** and we nearly **STARVED TO DEATH**. All thanks to Scout Master Geoffrey, who was about as sharp as a soggy biscuit.

Summer camp was in the Lake District. I could only assume this was one big place full of lakes, where we could go swimming and boating.

I was a little *worried* as I've had some mishaps camping next to water. So imagine my surprise (and relief) when we turned up and were in the middle of a deer-infested forest!

What on EARTH were we going to do here?!

Bird-watch?

Deer-watch?

Tree-watch?

It did make me feel better to see lots of other kids from school there though. There was **NITTY NEIL** (who used to have nits, but now he has a massive zit on his nose, so we'll have to call him **ZITTY** Neil) and Belinda, Amy Almond - who's a welder and is best friends with the freakishly strong Debra Derby - Leo, Michael and a few others.

Debra Derby wasn't there.

Amy said she was in Italy with her mum, Diesel Doris, who was competing in the **EUROPEAN LORRY RACING CHAMPIONSHIPS** . . .

I was disappointed that Debra wasn't camping with us.

But not because she's **LOVELY** or anything . . . just because she's really, erm, COOL. And her mum drives a lorry.

Anyway . . .

We hopped off the bus and found out we were staying in LOG CABINS. This seemed awesome, especially considering my DISASTROUS experiences with tents!

I'd just started to think that this camp may not be so bad after all until I saw . . . **WAIT** for it

. . . Can you guess?

You got it!

Smug, full-of-himself, twit-faced Gareth
Trumpshaw.

Typical. He'd brought loads of sophisticated
camping gadgets with him (his Dad probably made
them for him). He's such a **TWIT**.

To make matters worse, he was put in the same cabin as us . . . well, for a bit.

Fortunately Superdog found a dead mouse in the corner of our cabin and Percy **THREW UP**. Gareth complained and got moved to another cabin.

RESULT!!!

Our camp leader is, thankfully, miles better than Scout Master Geoffrey! His name is Stewart. Or as we call him . . . PSYCHO STU!

Psycho Stu is Scottish. He is really tall and strong. He has long, red wavy hair and he always wears a kilt.

Apparently he has 'survival skills' (whatever that means) so we'll be doing lots of fun, outdoor activities whilst we're in the Lake District.

Anyway, Psycho Stu took us fishing on the first day. His idea of fishing isn't what we're used to.

He said that to survive in nature, we all had to learn to catch fish with our BARE HANDS. Gareth complained because he'd brought along a high-tech fishing rod he wanted to use.

Stu didn't let Gareth use it though.

I mean, I didn't rate my chances of catching dinner with my bare hands, but I was chuffed that Gareth was in a **SNOT**.

None of the kids at camp succeeded in catching any fish, but Stu was a natural. He caught everyone's dinner. That was the awesome part.

After that he decided to teach us all how to **GUT A FISH**. This was the less awesome part.

Not surprisingly, Percy was **SICK**.

I think a few other kids wanted to be sick too,
but Percy was first.

Typical.

The next day Stu took us to learn to shoot a bow and arrow.

Both Percy and I thought this was perfect tactical training that could come in really handy when I – err – I mean WE go to work for **METAL FACE**.

Gareth had brought his own laser-guided bow and arrow, but Stu didn't let him use it.

Gareth wasn't happy.

As it turns out Stu was **REALLY GOOD** at shooting an arrow, but he wasn't as good at controlling a camp full of kids who just wanted to shoot each other.

I shot an arrow and it went *REALLY FAR!!!* All the way into a nearby camp!

Now, I don't know what Stu's problem was, but I can't see why we should be worried about 'BOOT CAMP'.

I mean, a camp for boots?! What a STUPID idea!

When we got back to camp Psycho Stu made a fire.

He was trying to teach us how to do it, but he decided that we weren't allowed to help after Percy managed to set fire to his own socks.

Stu told us we had to keep the fire going all day and all night, so somebody would always have to be on

FIRE DUTY.

As it turned out, fire duty meant going to collect sticks and throwing them on the fire . . .

This was not our idea of AWESOME.

In fact, it was about as much fun as our last camp's potato peeling duty . . .

z^{zzzz}

We got bored after a while and went to investigate the nearby Boot Camp.

I didn't see any boots, but I did hear a lot of military style shouting. In fact, if I didn't know better, I could have sworn that I heard Ms Mills' voice. (Ms Mills is our VERY SCARY P.E. teacher. Mr Hammond, the science teacher is even more scared of her than we are!)

After that Percy and I killed some time making bets on when exactly Zitty Neil's **giant zit** would **EXPLODE**, and on how many people it would take with it.

This was quite good fun until Percy came over all white and **PUKED** on the campfire.

(Why, Percy? . . . **WHY?**)

We were taken off campfire duty after that.

Psycho Stu also tried to get us to make our own
shelters, every night.

This didn't stop Stu though. Percy, Superdog and I were pretty impressed by his efforts.

By the end of the week, his shelter had an indoor fireplace with a chimney, a bed and a pantry (full of the **DEAD THINGS** he'd caught).

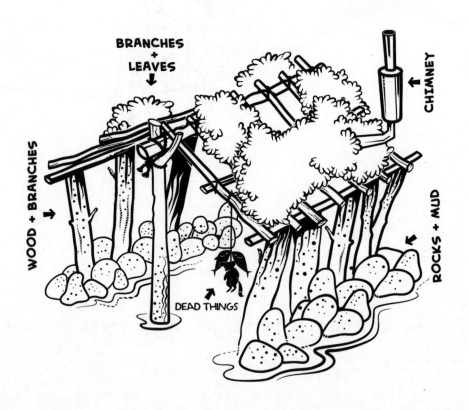

BRANCHES
+
LEAVES

CHIMNEY

WOOD + BRANCHES

ROCKS + MUD

DEAD THINGS

We took some notes for any future shelter-building we might have to do, although our shelters will have to have a place for Percy to be **SICK** in, especially if we're going to keep anything **DEAD** in there.

With all this EXCITEMENT, I'd managed to forget two very important things:

1)   That I hadn't had **ANY** time to look for super-cool finds

2)   My arch-nemesis, smug, full-of-himself, twit-faced Gareth Trumpshaw, was also at camp, and we hadn't tried to sabotage him even ONCE! (how could I forget THAT??)

Percy and I decided to trek through the woods a bit and see if we could discover any **fantastic finds.**

This was mainly to avoid Gareth, who was showing off his new gadget-compass/watch that his dad had made him.

He was doing this behind Psycho Stu's back of course, as Stu really didn't like Gareth's **_HIGH-TECH_** gadgets.

I couldn't wait to show Gareth what my dad had made me (baked-bean and eel jelly) in the form of a **HUGE FART**.

56

Superdog didn't want to come with us on our expedition. He had a date with that **DEAD MOUSE.**

We didn't unearth too many interesting finds in the forest:

-   Acorns

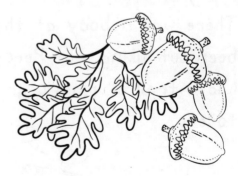

-   Lots of leaves

-   Some more leaves

\-   A few sticks

\-   Mud

\-   An old tennis ball

\-   A lake (But obviously, we couldn't bring the lake back with us, although it was good to know that there were actually lakes in the LAKE District.)

We didn't feel that we'd found the right material to make any 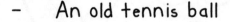 inventions in the forest, so Percy and I crept into the nearby **'Boot Camp'**. There was nobody at the camp, they must have been out hiking, but Percy and I found that they had a trail of plastic glow sticks leading to their toilets.

This **must** be how they found their way to and from the toilets at night.

We thought it would be fun to move a few glow sticks and make a trail from their camp to Gareth's cabin.

We couldn't think of what to make with the rest of our finds, this stuff wasn't quite what we needed to make something cool.

Instead, like any good superhero (I'm **EXPERIMENTAL FACE** . . . remember??) we used our ~~inishetiv~~ ~~inititinesh~~ **BRAINS** and made disguises.

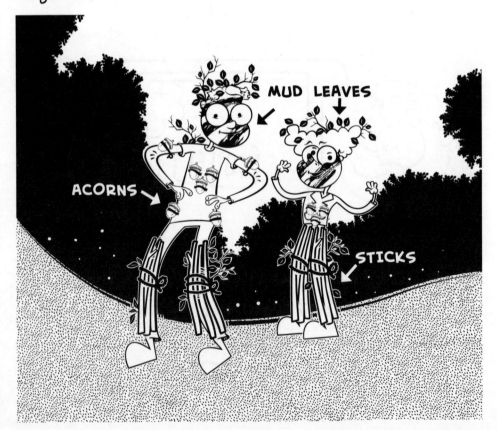

MUD LEAVES

ACORNS

STICKS

We realised pretty quickly that our disguises were *pointless*.

Although, we did manage to scare Zitty Neil and Leo into thinking there was a **GHOST** throwing a tennis ball and acorns around camp.

As it turns out, the next activity was to go hunting.

Psycho Stu was **REALLY IMPRESSED** with the disguises, he said that they were perfect camouflage, and he congratulated us on paying attention when he said we'd be going hunting.

Actually, neither Percy nor I had been listening when he told us about the hunting, but we got congratulated and Gareth look , especially after Stu told him he couldn't use his military-grade camouflage suit.

RESULT!!

Stu was really **HYPED** about the hunting trip (he hunts and cooks all of his own food, apparently); he told us that for dinner we'd only be allowed to eat what we hunted.

I had a bit of a bad feeling about this, but we didn't have a lot of choice.

Stu made the whole group disguise themselves, and off we went to find dinner.

Stu and Superdog seemed to be the **ONLY** people enjoying this.

Superdog caught flies and rolled around in the mud a lot, and Stu managed to harpoon a few rats and a badger.

I think we had a bit of a **disadvantage**. We weren't allowed bows and arrows, rifles or any other useful hunting weapons.

We were allowed to use the harpoons that we were supposed to make out of a branch and sharpen to a point.

ObviousLy everyone had got bored of sharpening sticks, so no one had a harpoon . . . apart from Gareth, who had a heat-seeking harpoon that his Dad had made and that Stu wouldn't let him use.

As the afternoon progressed and we started to get hungry, I think we were all thinking the same thing: "I hope there's enough badger to go around".

That is, everyone except Superdog, I could see him eyeing up those **DEAD RATS** . . .

The rodents didn't really go down too well in the end.

Everybody spent the whole night with **BAD STOMACHS**, and kept having to run to the toilet.

I managed to get out of it by only pretending to eat the roast badger, and scoffing Dad's baked-bean and eel jelly instead.

It wasn't long before we ran out of toilet paper, so it was just as well that Psycho Stu taught us that leaves are good for wiping your bottom.

That was pretty useful seeing as we'd collected so many earlier in the day.

Maybe not the **POISON IVY** leaves though, Percy found that out the hard way.

With all that chaos, it took a while before anyone noticed that we'd been **INVADED.**

Our glow stick trick had worked!

People from next door's "Boot Camp" had started following the trail of glow sticks in the dark in search of the toilets and had been using Gareth's cabin instead.

RESULT!!!

The first activity the next day was Horse Riding.

Most of us had been horse riding at least a couple of times. Amy Almond was a natural.

Stu assured us that the horses were all really tame, but Gareth said that it didn't matter, because he had a **special helmet** that allowed him to control the horse's mind with TELEPATHY.

Stu didn't let him use it.

Gareth wanted to ride at the front as if he were leading an expedition. Percy and I decided to stay behind. This way we could enjoy the view of Gareth's horse dragging him off the path, nibbling at things and walking under all the low branches, which kept **HITTING** him in the face.

It was **HILARIOUS!**

Then, the next activity was *canoeing*.

It was two people per boat, so me and Percy hopped in one and started rowing out onto the lake. Leo and Michael followed, and then Zitty Neil and Belinda.

Gareth refused to get in a canoe with anyone (because he's a TWIT), so Amy had to go with Psycho Stu.

We could hardly keep up!

To be honest — I started to feel like I was in P.E class, what with all of the 'OUTDOOR ACTIVITIES' we'd been doing, and now this.

I had a feeling Psycho Stu might somehow be in league with Miss Mills (my P.E teacher!).

But actually canoeing did turn out **OK**. Well, it was ok if you ignore the fact that there turned out to be more swimming involved than we'd initially counted on.

Percy and I didn't really see the point in paddling properly, mostly we just got really distracted and starting splashing each other with water.

But when we saw Michael and Leo 𝕤𝕥𝕣𝕒𝕟𝕕𝕖𝕕 with their paddles floating away, we decided to help.

It was what any good superhero would do . . .

We paddled (s l o w l y) over to them, and told Leo to hold onto the back of our canoe. But with two canoes, it was hard to actually move anywhere.

So instead, we gave them one of our paddles – but actually that meant that we both just started spinning round in circles instead of actually moving anywhere.

We decided that the **ONLY SOLUTION** would be to all get in one canoe, so we'd have two paddles.

We all managed to pile into one canoe, and we left the other one drifting in the middle of the lake. As I was saying, this seemed like the **perfect solution** . . .

UNTIL WE STARTED TO SINK.

We had no choice but to **ABANDON SHIP** and swim back to shore.

The man we hired the canoes from was pretty annoyed that two of his canoes were stranded in the lake . . . but it was clearly HIS fault for not giving us enough paddles.

Anyway, it could have been worse.

Well, maybe . . .

On the last night we sat around the campfire, and Stu told us a story about the woods.

Psycho Stu: You know, there is a **MYSTICAL CREATURE** that lives in these woods . . .

Smug, full-of-himself, twit-faced Gareth Trumpshaw snorted and said there were no **MYSTERIOUS CREATURES** living in England.

Gareth: This is **ENGLAND**, if there were any mysterious creatures the scientists would know about them!

Psycho Stu: **Oh yeah?!?!** You see many scientists camping in these woods?

Psycho Stu looked back at the rest of us, determined to tell his story.

Psycho Stu: Many years ago, on a dark, cold, rainy
night, I was camping in these very woods . . . it
was late, and I was running out of firewood.
I made my way through the woods by the light
of a HANDMADE TORCH in search of any
dry timber. From the pitch-black forest, I heard
rustling behind some bushes . . .

Everyone

h e l d

    t h e i r

        b r e a t h

as we listened to the story.

Gareth: Hang on . . . how did the torch stay lit if it was raining?

Psycho Stu: **DiD I SAY YOU COULD ASK QUESTIONS?**

Anyway, I approached the bushes and hid . . . and there he was . . . before my very eyes –

BiGFOOT!!

WE ALL GASPED.

But **twitty** Gareth was quick to interrupt:

Gareth: That makes no sense! If it was dark, and you had a torch . . . THE ONLY LIGHT SOURCE IN THE DARK FOREST . . . how come Bigfoot didn't run away?

Psycho Stu: Gareth, I think you're going to be on fish-gutting duty tomorrow . . .

Personally I think Gareth was just being **smug** and **full-of-himself.**

He'd **HATED** most of camp because Stu was more interested in hunting than in things that Gareth liked. That wasn't hard though, seeing as the only things Gareth likes are:

1)   Homework

2)   Homework

3)   Getting As on his homework

4)   Cheating on his homework (probably)

5)   All the high-tech gadgets that Stu wouldn't let him use

Gareth hadn't noticed that Superdog had crept up to him.

He must have been **PRETTY ANNOYED** with Gareth, because he climbed onto his shoulder and he stuck his **TONGUE** in Gareth's **EAR**.

I mean, it's also possible that Supedog had spotted a **JUICY MOTH** hovering around Gareth . . . either way, Gareth wasn't happy.

Percy laughed with everyone else for about two minutes (until he saw Superdog chewing the moth). Then he turned a **HORRIBLE SHADE OF GREEN** and – you guessed it – he was **SICK**.

Once we'd got Superdog's tongue out of Gareth's ear, we prepared to go to bed.

Stu packed a satchel full of **DEAD THINGS** he'd caught and prepared to disappear into the forest. He said he was 'going to see an old friend'.

Clearly he was going to see **BIGFOOT**. I was a bit jealous.

Anyway, camp was pretty cool in the end.

We almost felt sad having to leave Psycho Stu. Some of his survival skills could come in REALLY HANDY during a Superhero-type adventure.

We were back in Greenville the next day. I was **pretty pleased** to get back to reality so I could work on my inventions.

Metal Face can't create all of his gadgets by himself you know!!

I'd also **HAD ENOUGH** of Gareth. Although we managed to keep out of each other's way (sort of), having your ARCH-NEMESIS around **ALL THE TIME** can be pretty annoying.

Anyway, when we got back, it turned out Dad had finished his **SUPER-STRONG FART POTION** too. **BONUS!**

He said Percy and I could try it, but only after tea so that Mum wouldn't **kick us out** of the house for farting at the table.

It looked AWESOME.

He said it was made from a combination of:

This seemed like Dad's BEST creation yet.

After tea, we ran up to the ~~SUPER-SECRET LAB~~ CLUBHOUSE, and scoffed the jelly. Dad said to take it easy and not to eat too much, what with it being so **SUPER-STRONG**.

So we didn't eat too much. Well, not **ALL** of it anyway.

We waited.   And waited.

And then just when I thought it wasn't going to happen . . .

Percy let out a

HUMONGOUS FART.

And then I did too!!

They were so HUGE, that all of the jam jars in the clubhouse rattled and the leaves in the trees started SHAKING.

Dad came running out waving his hands in the air like a bit of a **Lunatic** and shouting **'I'VE DONE IT!'** over and over.

Mum **wasn't** very impressed. Apparently some of the neighbours had come out of their houses to see if there had been an **EARTHQUAKE**.

Anyway, we were pretty lucky that Dad managed to get his fart potion finished, because whilst we were away he got a **PROMOTION!!**

He got hired a few months ago by a **REALLY IMPORTANT** company that make camping gear and sportswear. It's called **CAMP-WEAR**.

Dad was **MEANT** to be inventing new things and improving their products.

FAAART...

The first week **didn't go too well**. He poured some of his experimental fart potion into one of the company's best flasks . . . and the potion melted it.

Unfortunately Dad had already drunk some of the potion when he was trying on one of the company's newly designed wet suits: that's how he managed to blow a hole in it.

During that week he also set fire to a frying pan and ⦚ a fishing boat.
SANK

Apparently it's **not** a good idea to use gunpowder to light a campfire on a fishing boat while it's floating in the water.

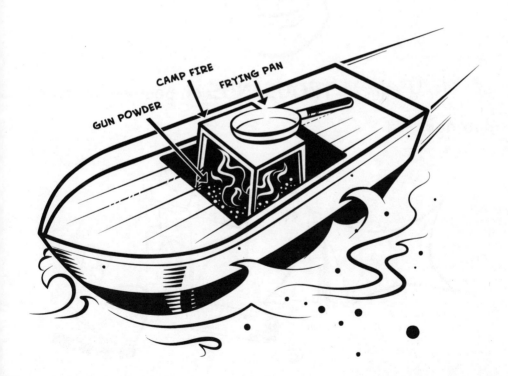

We were all pretty sure that Dad would get the sack for two **really good** reasons:

-   He hadn't **ACTUALLY** invented anything

-   He'd caused **THOUSANDS** of pounds worth of damage

So we were all **REALLY SURPRISED** when his boss gave him a promotion!

His boss said that, in all his experience, no one had ever put their products to the test like my Dad had, and he gave him his own department.

My Dad is now Head of the

DISASTER AREA.

The company sealed off a room where Dad spends all day **WRECKiNG** things.

He can flood, sink, burn down or blow up ABSOLUTELY ANYTHING he likes all in the name of research . . .

He's not very good when it comes to mending things, but when it comes to DESTROYING stuff, he's a natural.

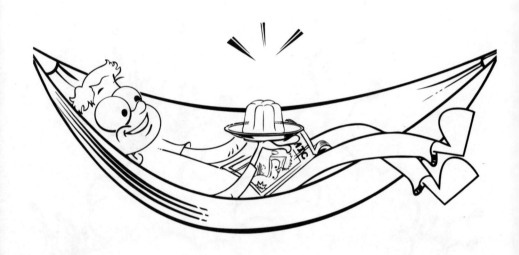

So with Dad at work all day and Mum busy with Mel and her tarot card reading, I thought I would be able to spend my days in absolute **bliss**, doing all those things I'd WANTED to do before Mum made me go to camp.

BUT NO . . .

Mum informed me that I had to go to the Sci-Fi Convention with Grandad Leonard and Granny Jean.

I know that *some kids* get bored of hanging out with their grandparents, but this wasn't *as* bad as it sounded.

Grandad Leonard is about as COOL as Dad when it comes to inventing things and being a **SUPER-GENIUS.**

And Granny Jean always looks **AWESOME** in her costumes. She's also pretty handy when it comes to martial arts, knitting and camouflage techniques.

Hopefully they could give me some COOL ideas about how to become an assistant to Metal Face!

We also had to dress up.

This is a **MUST** when you go to a Sci-Fi Convention.

Grandad Leonard and Granny Jean **ALWAYS** dress up, even when they're **NOT** going to a Sci-Fi Convention. (This can be a bit embarrassing when you're just popping down to the supermarket.)

Both Percy and I wanted to go as Metal Face.

But then we realised that **THE REAL METAL FACE** might be there, and we wouldn't want people to confuse us with him.

AWKWARD!!

So we decided to create our own costumes from our stash of **SUPER-COOL STUFF**.

We were really lucky, because when Dad was on his way home from work last week he noticed a skip outside a local pub that's being redecorated, so he had a snoop around and brought us some **FANTASTIC STUFF!**

LOOK AT THIS!! WHAT A FIND!!

He brought us **LOADS** of wood, picture frames, old door knobs, curtains, pots and pans, oil lamps and horse brasses.

OIL LAMP

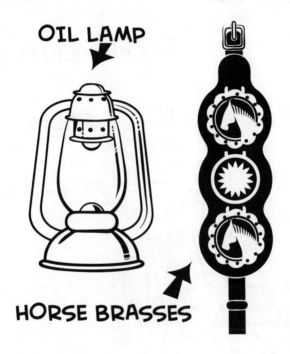

HORSE BRASSES

It was the perfect moment to finally design my **EXPERIMENTAL FACE** costume.

Percy decided to go for something a bit more 'Olde-Worldy' and used the horse brasses and the oil lamp. COOL or what?!

EXPERIMENTAL FACE

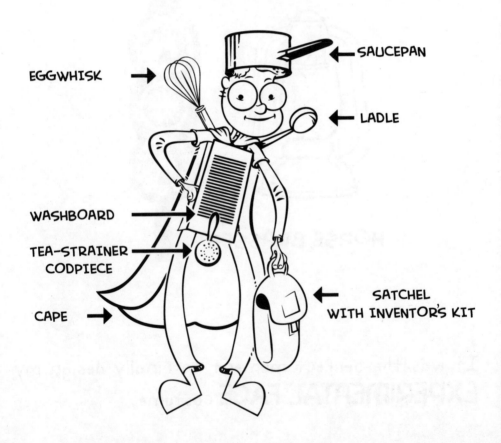

SAUCEPAN

EGGWHISK

LADLE

WASHBOARD

TEA-STRAINER CODPIECE

CAPE

SATCHEL WITH INVENTOR'S KIT

BRASS INVADER

MASK →

HORSE BRASSES
FOR COOLNESS →

LUCKY HORSESHOE
CODPIECE →

CAPE FOR
FLYING →

← OIL LAMP FOR
NIGHT VISION

Grandad Leonard thought our costumes were 'very creative' and even Mum said that we looked '**AMAZING**. Just . . . amazing . . .'

Mum: What Superheroes are you going as, may I ask?

Danny: I'm going as myself . . . the **MIGHTY EXPERIMENTAL FACE** . . . and Percy over there is **THE BRASS INVADER!**

Mum: Okay boys. Well, I think you're going to fit right in at a Sci-Fi Convention . . . (Mum with raised eyebrows)

I wonder what she meant by that . . .

I asked Mum if she would let me take Superdog, **AND SHE AGREED!** I didn't have to bribe her or anything. She said:

Mum: Yes, you might as well take him. I don't see how that can make things any worse.

RESULT!!

So, the Sci-Fi Convention was

FARTACULAR!!

Everybody was dressed up as aliens, mutants and superheroes.

Grandad Leonard and Granny Jean went as characters from their favourite TV show, Star Trip, like they always do.

Mum didn't let me take any fart potion because Granny Jean said 'I don't want him going off in the car'; but I had secretly **(GENIUSLY)** stashed some away for later.

Whilst Grandad Leonard and Granny Jean were talking to their friends, Percy and I got a lot of time to go and explore (and to scoff some **FART JELLY**).

We were pretty excited that we might be able to see **METAL FACE** again, but we tried to 'act cool'.

Percy ***DIDN'T QUITE*** pull it off.

Actually he spent most of the time hanging around outside the toilets. He was convinced that even Metal Face would have to go eventually and so this was the best place to spot him.

Also, **WITH ALL OUR FARTING**, being near the toilets was probably a good thing.

It was pretty lucky actually, because it was when we were hanging around the toilets that we heard about an awesome **COSTUME COMPETITION**.

It was going to start in an hour in the main hall, Percy and I looked at each other: first prize was **OURS!**

In the meantime, Superdog and I scoped out the stalls and decided to see if we could get our hands on some fantastic finds.

Lots of people seemed to be losing bits off of their costumes, so we managed to get our hands on some **COOL STUFF**.

We found:

PIN-BADGES

FEATHERS

LIZARD CONTACT LENS

FOAM HAMMER

FAKE ALIEN SCALES

PIRATE HAT

We **WEREN'T SURE** what inventions we could actually make from this. But I knew we'd come up with something.

Until then, we decided to let Superdog use them for a costume. He didn't have one after all, and he could join the costume competition then too.

It was as we were decorating Superdog's pirate hat that we saw him. We heard a **huge fart** and we turned around . . .

It was **HIM!!**

You know, **METAL FACE!!**

I looked at Percy . . .

        Percy looked at me . . .

we were both getting a bit sweaty and Percy looked rather **NAUSEOUS**.

He was stood at a stand full of **METAL FACE COMICS** and **METAL FACE MEMORIBILLIA**, talking to a ~~man woman/human~~ an **ALIEN** covered in bright purple fur.

I wondered if he was an **intergalactic nemesis**, or an **ally from another planet!!**

Either way, we trusted Metal Face to know what was going on . . . but we thought we'd better go and offer our help, just in case things got ugly with the purple fuzzy alien.

METAL FACE . . . YOUR HIGHNESS . . .

HUH? WHAT DO YOU WANT, KID?

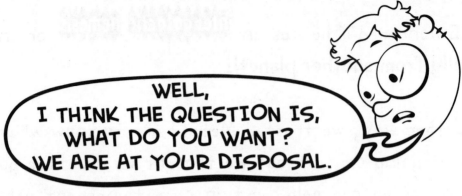

Then he did this big laugh (and a small fart), and the fuzzy alien joined in.

I knew there must be some kind of *emergency situation* in Spain that needed his help. So I gave him a salute and turned to Percy . . .

Who was **SICK**.

Why, Percy? . . . WHY?

I wanted to hang around to chat to Metal Face for a bit longer in order to get all the details of the secret **'SPANISH MISSION'**, but there was an announcement asking costume competition entrants to go to the main hall.

Percy and I ══ *DASHED OFF*.

We needed to go and pick up our award.

I mean, we hadn't won anything yet . . . but **HOW COULD WE LOSE?!**

Unfortunately though, we didn't win first place, or second . . . or third.

We did win a prize though: we won the trophy for **'The Most Outrageous Outfits'.**

I don't really know what "OUTRAGEOUS" means, but I won a tin of chocolates, so I don't care.

Grandad Leonard: That's strange, usually that prize goes to the **MOST RIDICULOUS** outfit.

Danny: Well, this year they've changed it!

I wasn't too bothered about not winning first place until I saw that the person who **HAD** won first place was none other than **MR. HAMMOND.**
MY SCIENCE TEACHER!

What was **HE** doing here?

Mr Hammond looked pretty pleased with himself. He was dressed as an astronaut with a thin, green scaly tail. **BORING!**

Mr Hammond saw us though and came over to chat. He mostly spoke to Grandad Leonard and Granny Jean.

They kept saying it was **'WONDERFUL'** that he had won and that his costume really was **VERY ORIGINAL AND EXCITING'**.

I pretended I was fine with him winning instead of us, but I think he caught on to me . . .

Percy didn't clock on to my plan. So I stamped on his foot . . .

It got a bit AWKWARD.

Percy kept moaning about his toe.

We were all about to leave when a lady got up to
the stage and distracted everyone.

NOW, AS YOU ALL KNOW,
EVERY YEAR GREENVILLE
TOWN HALL
AND COSMIC COMICS
ORGANISE A COMPETITION
AT THE END OF THE SUMMER.
THE COMPETITION IS TO
BUILD A FLYING MACHINE.
THE MACHINES WILL BE
LAUNCHED OFF
GREENVILLE PIER
ON THE 21ST OF AUGUST
AND THE ONE THAT STAYS
IN THE AIR THE LONGEST
WILL BE THE WINNER.

FLYING MACHINE?!

Like, **A JET?**

JUST LIKE METAL FACE ASKED FOR!!

It was **FATE.**

I grabbed Percy's shoulders and shouted:

The lady on stage looked at me crossly.

Grandad Leonard and Granny Jean shuffled about a bit.

And Mr Hammond turned around like he didn't know us.

Percy let out a tiny, squeaky **FART**. I think that diffused the tension a bit.

Or at least, it distracted the lady's attention from me . . .

The lady scowled and then got off the stage to hand out leaflets.

Mr Hammond took one (and said thank you when she 'congratulated' him).

Mr Hammond: This is great, boys. It's a shame that there's no science club during the summer holidays, it would be such a fun project . . .

Grandad Leonard: It would be such a good project for the boys!

Granny Jean: Oh look! The prize is a family trip to Spain. I could do with a holiday.

So when we got home, it was settled. Percy, Superdog, Grandad Leonard and I would work on the **flying machine** together.

Mum had done a **BBQ** for us when we got back, so we took this as the **PERFECT OPPORTUNITY** to start making plans.

UnfortunateLy, Mr Hammond had come back with us.

I don't know why.

Grandad Leonard had asked him to join us.

He said he had found a **'kindred spirit'** because Mr Hammond was just as interested in sci-fi as he was.

I don't know what that means, but Granny Jean kept rolling her eyes when Grandad Leonard and Mr Hammond weren't looking, so I can only assume it was a **BAD THING**.

Either way, she seemed just as annoyed as me.

Now, I don't really have anything against Mr Hammond (apart from the way he ROBBED us of first place in the costume competition).

I mean, Mr Hammond is **PRETTY COOL** as teachers go. And he's my science teacher, so he already rates pretty high on my coolness scale.

But it's the SUMMER. Why would I want my TEACHER hanging around and coming to BBQ's...? It's not like all those sausages weren't going to get eaten...

This is bad enough, RIGHT? Well, hang on for this because it gets worse!

Grandad Leonard turned around to Mr Hammond and said:

Grandad: You know? It would be great if you could help us build the flying machine, I'm sure the boys would love it . . .

I was GOBSMACKED!!!

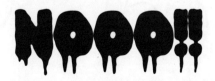

Percy seemed pleased.

Percy: That would be brilliant!!!

So I threatened to tread on his toes again.

Great! Thanks **GRANDAD!!** Now I have to spend all summer with my TEACHER!

It was too late to change the course of events:

I knew I'd just have to get used to the idea of Mr Hammond hanging around and (worst of all) SNOOPING around my Secret Lab . . .

I mean, CLUBHOUSE.

After the **BBQ**, we set to work making plans for the flying machine, which I had now named

THE JET OF JUSTICE

Grandad Leonard started talking about LASERS and ROCKET-FUEL.

Mr Hammond said we should think 'practical'.
I scowled at Mr Hammond, even though I secretly

agreed that LASERS probably weren't the first

priority.

Anyway, we agreed to meet at the **clubhouse** again on Sunday morning to start work.

Percy and I spent the rest of the week preparing for the first JET OF JUSTICE team meeting.

We thought it would be pretty helpful to make some plans so that our flying machine would be the **BESTFLYING MACHINE EVER.**

We knew that a lot of tin foil would be needed to make it look SLEEK and **AWESOME.**

We were in the clubhouse drawing diagrams of jet engines when Dad got home. He wanted to check on our progress and give us some of his most recent fart-jelly.

He said it was based on his most recent batch, you know, the SUPER-STRONG FART POTION he had been working on.

This one had an extra special ingredient in it though.

We thought it was best not to ask about that...

I could already tell it was going to be a good one. He'd been working on it for a while.

Dad was now able to work on some of his potions

from his lab at work. Apparently, none of his colleagues ever dared enter Dad's "Disaster Area" for fear of being **blown-up**.

Dad revealed the *jelly* like it was a precious treasure.

Percy and I looked at each other, and then we looked at Dad.

He looked particularly pleased with himself already.

Dad: Now boys, be very careful with this jelly, a little bit will go a long way.

Percy and I tried a tiny spoonful each, then waited . . .

I could hear Percy's stomach **RUMBLiNG**. Mine was rumbling too!

Only seconds later our bottoms exploded! We both did the

BIGGEST FART I HAVE EVER HEARD!!!

It was the kind of fart that could rival **METAL FACE** himself!

The clubhouse SHOOK.

The trees SHOOK.

A few garden gnomes fell over.

And the water started **sloshing** around in the bird bath.

It was **AWESOME**.

SO awesome that Mum came running into the garden to see what was going on.

Dad looked really proud. He should look proud!

Percy and I both agreed that he had created **GENIUS-LEVEL** jelly!

Mum: Was that a tornado? A hailstorm?

Dad: No, it was . . .err . . .

Mum: Oh, never mind. I'm sure I can guess what it was!

Mum: Can't you just **BEHAVE?** I'm trying to do a **READING!**

Mum had just started her own tarot card reading business.

I'm pretty sure the cards didn't predict our

AWESOME FART.

Although so far, apparently they had predicted the death of Mr Jones's hamster and Mrs Henry's skiing accident.

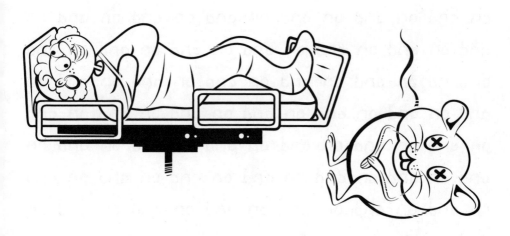

They also managed to predict that I would fail Maths again, and that I'd be grounded for a month . . . WEIRD, Huh?

Anyway, Mum had been going on and on. . . and on about some freak weather coming soon.

That hadn't happened yet.

But she'd 'seen it in her cards', and her cards were pretty good at predicting some things (like my bad grades).

I guess that probably explains why she'd been on edge all week worrying about sudden **THUNDERSTORMS OR TORNADOES.**

ANYWAY . . .

On Sunday, Mr Hammond turned up with Grandad Leonard, so we officially started work on the **JET OF JUSTICE**.

Granny Jean couldn't make it.

Apparently she told Grandad Leonard that he didn't need her anymore, now that he'd found a new 'kindred spirit'.

I felt pretty annoyed that Mr. Hammond got to see my super-secret laboratory **CLUBHOUSE**.

This place was reserved for **SUPER- INVENTORS** and people who would be helpful when making gadgets.

I mean, what if he told somebody about the **SECRETS** it contained and my **GENIUS INVENTIONS?**

What if smug, full-of-himself, twit-faced Gareth Trumpshaw found out about what we did up here?

WHAT IF **METAL FACE** DECIDED OUR POSITION WAS COMPROMISED AND NEVER ACCEPTED ME AS HIS **SUPER-INVENTOR** SIDEKICK!?

I decided that desperate measures had to be taken.
I wouldn't let Mr. Hammond in until he PROMISED
not to tell anyone about the clubhouse.

I couldn't take **ANY CHANCES.**

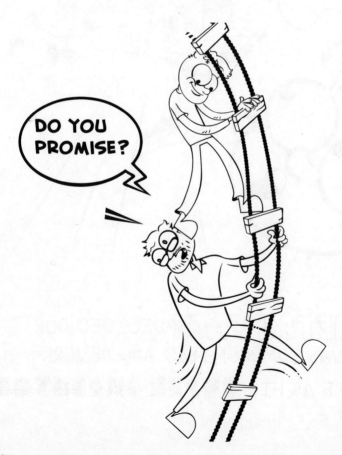

He thought I was joking at first.

But then I told him if he didn't promise, I would let Superdog lick his nose.

I PROMISE! I PROMISE!

Mr. Hammond seemed pretty impressed by the **clubhouse** in the end though, so I felt a bit better about him being allowed to help.

I suppose his science knowledge could be useful too, seeing as Percy and I had only got as far as the tin foil part of the design before Dad distracted us with his amazing fart jelly.

Grandad Leonard and Mr Hammond were getting started drawing up some **BLUEPRINTS** for the

JET OF JUSTICE.

Dad didn't seem very pleased about this.

In fact, Dad hadn't seemed very pleased since we'd decided that Mr Hammond could help us. I don't know why. Maybe it was because Mr Hammond could do lots of things Dad couldn't, like:

-Actually invent stuff instead of destroying it

-Draw blueprints

-Some other stuff, although I don't know what

Just when it was getting a bit heated, and Dad was trying to show Mr Hammond the best way to sharpen a pencil . . .

. . . Percy revealed some very bad news.

Apparently he had found out that Gareth Trumpshaw and his dad would be entering the competition!

This was a **DISASTER!!**

I mean, I **TOTALLY** believed that we could beat him;

I knew that the prize was as good as ours – but Gareth Trumpshaw is a **TOTAL TWIT** and a **CHEAT**.

In fact, he's a big, **fat-headed** cheaty **TWIT** and his Dad always helps him with cutting edge technology from his work.

This was really **BAD NEWS**!!

Steam was literally coming out of Dad's ears. Dad dislikes Gareth's Dad just as much as I dislike Gareth.

Dad thinks that Gareth's Dad was responsible for him losing his job at Acmetech.

In reality, knowing Dad's work, I'd have to guess that Dad was definitely capable of setting fire to the factory on his own without **ANYONE'S** help or influence.

BUT Gareth's Dad is a smug, full-of-himself **TWIT** too, so I figured I wouldn't mention this to Dad.

Dad: Those Trumpshaw twits are going to be cheating, using all the latest cutting edge technology, and what do we have? TIN FOIL!

Percy and I looked at each other. We couldn't understand what Dad suddenly had against tin foil.

Thankfully, Mr Hammond came to the rescue.
Mr Hammond:

NOW REALLY,
I DON'T THINK WE NEED 'CUTTING EDGE' TECHNOLOGY TO WIN. WE JUST NEED TO CREATE SOMETHING STREAMLINED.

I wasn't sure what 'streamline' meant, but I was hoping it didn't have anything to do with streams.

This seemed to make Dad **even angrier**, somehow. He declared that he would go out and try to find materials whilst we worked on the design.

Well, whilst Grandad Leonard and Mr Hammond worked on the design.

Percy, Superdog and I decided to keep thinking about decoration (which was also **VERY** important).

Before they started though, I gave them the diagram Percy and I had drawn up.

It looked like this:

Mr Hammond and Grandad Leonard said it was **'VERY AMBITIOUS'** but that they would do the best they can.

Anyway, getting back to the decoration . . .

I still had lots of feathers from the **Sci-Fi** Convention, but Superdog **THREW UP** on them.

And then Percy threw up too.

Why, Percy, **WHY?!**

Superdog was right though. Feathers weren't right for this.

So we raided the jam jars and tubs with all of our fantastic finds and came up with:

- Tin foil (of course)

- Pin badges (found at the Sci-Fi Convention)

- Fairy lights (borrowed from Mum's Christmas decorations box)

- Paper clips

- Glow sticks (we brought them back from camp)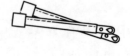

- Masking tape

- Chewed up chewing gum (I like to save it, it comes in handy . . . even though it always makes Percy sick)

If we wanted to make our jet **AWESOME** enough for Metal Face to take notice, we would have to work **HARD**.

Even though Grandad and Mr Hammond were working on the **BLUEPRINTS**, we decided to get ahead a bit by thinking of ways to make the engine.

Well, I say **"MAKE"** ...

But what I mean is **'borrow'**.

Because Percy and I had decided the best thing to do was to **'borrow'** an engine from someone, or something, else.

I mean, making a **WHOLE ENGINE** from scratch seemed a bit far-fetched.

The competition was only **ONE WEEK** away after all.

And naturally, as I am a SUPER-GENIUS, I'd had a really great idea.

We snuck into the shed looking for something with a spare engine and wheeled out Dad's lawn mower.

WE WEREN'T REALLY SURE HOW TO GET THE ENGINE OFF OF THE LAWN MOWER AND ONTO OUR JET. SO WE JUST HACKED AWAY AT IT UNTIL ALL OF THE PLASTIC LAWN MOWER BITS FELL OFF.

We put them safely back in the shed so that someone could put it back together after the competition...

It was only when we took the engine up to the laboratory clubhouse that Mr Hammond told us the jet wouldn't need an engine.

Percy and I were gutted... What kind of JET doesn't need an ENGINE?

And then he said that the jet would have to be pushed off of the pier by Percy and I.

Then, if the design was right, it would fly by itself. I wasn't happy about this. I'm more of a pilot than a **pusher**.

Dad was even less happy than me when he got back from looking for "MATERIALS".

Whilst I thought Dad wouldn't mind when I explained what we had tried to do, I knew Mum would probably go a little bit **MENTAL!!!!!**

Although I don't see why she should — she hardly **EVER** uses the lawn mower.

But she likes to make Dad use it a lot, especially when he's just blown-up the **DVD** player or melted the toilet seat.

So . . .

We hid the lawn mower parts, and the lawn mower engine, behind some of Dad's other tools in the shed.

Now that Mr Hammond had ruined our **FARTASTIC PLAN**, we decided to look at the design he and Grandad Leonard had drawn up.

I will be honest: it was nowhere near as good as mine and Percy's. Absolutely no flames **ANYWHERE**.

Dad had come back with some pretty awesome materials, so I was sure we could make Mr Hammond's design at least **LOOK** a bit better. (Probably.) Even if it wasn't really what we had in mind (at all) . . .

Dad had managed to raid a bunch of skips again.
He found:

← BUBBLE WRAP (LOTS OF IT!)

PLASTIC SHEETING ➡

← A FEW OLD LAMPSHADES

OLD CROQUET MALLETS ➡

← OLD CROQUET BALLS

OLD CROQUET HOOPS ➡

Using all this stuff, Grandad Leonard said he had a pretty idea of how he could make the wings of the jet. Although he was pretty disappointed that there was nothing he could make a phaser with.

Why is he **SO** obsessed with phasers???

Mr Hammond said he would start work on the wings with Grandad, and it was down to Dad, Percy, Superdog and I to find something to go underneath the wings that Percy and I could sit in.

He said it would need to be . . .

- Lightweight

- **Big enough** to carry us

- **Streamlined** (there's that phrase again?!)

- Have wheels so they could **PUSH** us down the pier

- **WATERPROOF**, if possible

First of all though, we had a game of croquet.

Well sort of. We didn't know how to play croquet
. . .

Or what the hoops were for . . .

Or how you scored points . . .

Or generally what the rules were . . .

SCORE

1	5	7	0
5	2	7	0
3	1	2	0

So we just hit the balls around a lot and gave each other points for the stuff we could hit in the garden.

It was all going well until Dad **KNOCKED** the head off of Mum's ornamental dragon.

We hid the evidence along with the bits of lawnmower and decided to get out of the garden whilst we still had the chance.

Finding a box/container/thing to hold Percy and me under the jet was **HARD WORK.**

First we thought a wheelie bin might do the job . . .

But Percy complained **SO MUCH** about me having to sit on his head that we had to forget that idea.

It probably didn't help that there was some mouldy cheese at the bottom of it.

Which made Percy **SICK**.

In the bin.

So we had to get rid of it anyway.

Next, Dad spotted a child's GO-KART ₀ ₀ ₀

This one was **SUPER-FUN**, but it wasn't very lightweight.

And we had a strong suspicion that it might belong to someone . . .

In the end though, we found something we thought could be pretty useful.

Well, Dad thought it was anyway.

I wasn't sure yet.

But when Percy and I sat in it, we knew it was **PERFECT**.

It was a **SHOPPING TROLLEY**.

It had been in the corner of the clubhouse all along, and none of us had noticed it because it was so full of junk . . . I mean, **Fantastic Finds**!

We emptied it out, then decided to test it by rolling each other down the hill for a bit, and we showed Grandad Leonard and Mr Hammond.

So they weren't QUITE as impressed as we had been.

But Mr Hammond said it would be light enough to attach to the wings, so that was a bonus.

Percy and I set to work decorating the shopping trolley whilst Dad helped Mr Hammond (who Grandad was now calling 'Henry'. **GROSS!**) and Grandad Leonard build the frame.

The shopping trolley was already **SUPER SHINY**, so we put the tin foil to one side for a bit.

Instead, we wrapped **bubble wrap ALL OVER** the handle, frame and sides and secured it with masking tape.

Then we hung the pin badges on some string and tied it to the front.

I scouted some old fairy lights I'd "**BORROWED**" from Mum's Christmas decoration box and wrapped them in and out of the sides.

Finally we **dangled** glow sticks from the wings with string and paper clips.

Overall, it was looking **PRETTY FARTACULAR.**

Metal Face would be able to spot us from MILES AWAY.

Looks a bit like a dodgy, flying PINATA.

We even padded down the front of the trolley so that Superdog would be able to pilot the jet (naturally, he has a pilot's license).

PILOT'S LICENSE

NAME: SUPERDOG
SPECIES: DOG TOAD
AGE: TOP SECRET

****
****1564

I was starting to get pretty excited about the competition now.

I mean, **WHAT COULD GO WRONG?!**

We had an awesome trolley, the best pilot in Greenville and **THREE SUPER-COOL INVENTORS** working on the wings.

Our plan was FOOL-PROOF.

Anyway, after all of this **HARD WORK**, we decided to 'call it a day' and meet up again soon to finish off.

Mr Hammond, or 'Henry', got a lift back with Grandad, after politely declining Mum's offer to have tea with us.

I don't blame him, it's usually REALLY HEALTHY.

Which actually means **REALLY BORING**.

And what on earth is Quinoa, anyway? Whatever happened to bacon butties?

Mum didn't seem very impressed when I tried to 'politely decline' tea too.

Okay, let me bring you up to speed!

The competition is only **TWO DAYS** away!!

We are putting the finishing touches on the mighty **JET OF JUSTICE**.

So, the jet isn't exactly looking as good as I planned. But Mr Hammond, Dad and Grandad Leonard are pretty sure it's going to fly.

It's also much bigger than we planned.

By much bigger, I mean it's

HUMONGOUS.

By humongous I mean we've had to **BREAK DOWN A WALL OF THE CLUBHOUSE** just to get it out.

Mum **WAS NOT** impressed.

But thankfully she's been too busy watching weather forecasts and running in and out of the garden checking for 'FREAK STORMS' to actually say anything about it.

Anyway, I'd been feeling a bit disappointed with the Jet of Justice, but actually, when we got it out of the clubhouse it looked more AWESOME than I had thought!

Grandad Leonard said we'll need to wear helmets when we actually fly in the jet.

So Percy and I are working on decorating our bike helmets — we have to match after all . . .

So far, we have added:

- **Bubble wrap** (of course)

- A bit of **TIN FOIL**

- **Leaves** (for camouflage)

- Glow sticks (for visibility)

We've also prepared a small tin foil pilot's hat for Superdog.

He seemed thrilled with it . . .

But he managed to ruin it by rolling around in a sludge pile at the bottom of the garden.

He came back covered in green goo and with bits of slug around his mouth.

Percy was **SICK**, on his helmet . . .

TYPICAL

THE DAY OF THE COMPETITION IS HERE!!!

We have been putting the final touches on the jet **ALL MORNING**, and we are finally ready to go.

It took us a while to attach the jet to Grandad's car.

But thankfully, I am a **GENIUS**, and I managed to think of a **BRILLIANT** way to get it to the competition safely.

Percy and I attached rope to the trolley and tied it to Grandad's bumper.

He didn't seem convinced.

IN FACT, he said:

Grandad Leonard: I'm not sure Danny, this looks even more dangerous than one of your Dad's ideas.

ACTUALLY, it had been Dad's idea. But we didn't tell Grandad that . . .

There was no time for arguments, though, because we were already meant to be at the competition.

Anyway, Grandad drove us **REALLY SLOWLY** to the pier.

So slowly, that a couple of seagulls sat on top of
the wings and took a nap.

When we arrived at the pier, Percy and I put on our helmets (and our raincoats – Mum's orders) and helped push our jet down to the queue of flying machines that were waiting to dive off the edge.

It was a pretty good turn-out actually.

Nitty Neil and Belinda were there.

Nitty Neil **STILL** had that huge zit on his nose, so he was still Zitty Neil.

Neil and Belinda's flying machine looked EVEN WORSE than ours.

It was a huge plastic box attached to a ship's sail. I had **NO IDEA** how that would fly, but at least when they landed in the water they could sail nicely back to shore.

There was also a bunch of people from the **Sci-Fi** convention taking part.

Grandad Leonard said hello to them, and lots of them were **STILL** 'congratulating' Mr Hammond for winning the costume competition.

Humph . . .

To make matters worse, we were stood behind smug, full-of-himself, twit-faced Gareth Trumpshaw and smug, full-of-himself, twit-faced Trumpshaw senior (Gareth's dad).

I SCOWLED a lot, and pretended I hadn't noticed.

Mr Hammond, annoying as always, went to say hello to the twit-faced Trumpshaws and admired their machine.

WHY, HAMMOND, WHY?

I was getting pretty worried about Dad, he was going an odd shade of purple and I thought he might explode at any moment.

I mean, Gareth's jet did look pretty ~~impressive~~ interesting.

In fact, I'm almost certain it had **ACTUAL WINGS** from a jet.

Surely that's cheating?

I mean, Gareth **ALWAYS** cheats, so it wouldn't surprise me.

Anyway, my attention was diverted as the lady that had been at the Sci-Fi convention got up onto a little podium.

Lady: Welcome, everyone, to the annual Greenville flying machine competition!

People started to slowly clap, then the wind blew all of her papers off of the podium.

Lady: Err . . .yes, the weather is awfully bad today.

BUT, the show must go on. Good luck everybody, may the best team win!

And with that, the first flying machine rushed down the pier and launched off the edge!!

And took a nose-dive straight into the water . . .

Percy looked a little nervous.

So nervous, that he was starting to turn green.

I did the only sensible thing I could, which was to turn him around just in time so that he didn't puke over Superdog and I . . .

But he did get a bit on Mr Hammond.

Well, he got a lot on Mr Hammond . . .

I mean, he puked **ALL OVER** Mr Hammond.

Oops.

We watched a few of the flying machines take their plummet off of the pier.

None of them did very well.

They also had to suspend the competition for ten minutes when it started

CHUCKING IT DOWN

with rain.

Maybe they wouldn't have postponed, but the rain had started just as Zitty Neil and Belinda had taken their go.

They didn't fly, **AT ALL**.

In fact, they pretty much just dropped straight into the water.
dropped
dropped

But what with all the rain, their plastic box filled up pretty quickly and the whole thing sank.

As they were sinking, Neil's **GIGANTIC ZIT** burst . . . all over Belinda!

It was hilarious . . .and **DISGUSTING**.

Percy was probably sick. I wasn't looking at Percy, but this is just the sort of thing that makes him blow chunks.

They had to send out the lifeguard to get them out of the water.

Then Neil's nose had to be treated by a medical worker. Talk about excitement!

We hadn't expected all this sudden wind and rain. Maybe Mum was right about the freak weather after all . . . ?

We took shelter under the wings of our jet. We were all pretty impressed with how well they held up.

Mum, baby sister Mel and Granny Jean had come down to watch and had decided to take shelter inside a nice cosy café on the pier.

Granny Jean waved at us enthusiastically through the window.

Mum didn't wave — she was too busy frowning at the clouds and checking the wind speed meter she'd bought online.

To be fair to Mum, the wind **WAS** picking up as the competition went on.

Gareth's jet flying GARBAGE was up next, anyway. Percy and I prepared ourselves as we were straight after him.

We jumped in the trolley, making sure Superdog had

a good view at the front so he could pilot us, and waited for Gareth to **FAIL MISERABLY!!**

Which he would . . .

Because he's is a **twit**.

His dad was running around with a screw driver checking things, and then he handed Gareth a helmet and a pair of goggles.

It was looking unnervingly professional.

BUT, Mr Hammond said something to make us all feel better. (finally!)

Mr Hammond: In this wind, I don't think Gareth's jet will fly. Those wings look **VERY** heavy. RESULT!!

We stood with baited breath as Gareth's dad turned the propeller on the jet (**UGH!**) and pushed Gareth towards the edge of the pier.

THEN . . .

He dropped.

I mean, **HE DROPPED**

An **ALMIGHTY GUST OF WIND** swept over the pier and pretty much **PUSHED** Gareth nose first into the water. He didn't even get a chance to try and fly!!

AWESOME.

Gareth didn't look very impressed when he got out.

He looked **VERY WET AND VERY SLIMY**, and like a complete and utter cheating twit (which is how he usually looks).

But he **DID NOT** look impressed.

Gareth's dad ran up to the judging stand and starting waving his arms about saying they should be allowed another chance.

But the judges ignored him.

IN FACT, one of the judges told him to calm down, and that his jet was full of modern gadgets that shouldn't be used.

Then he kicked him off of their podium . . .

It can't be possible, but I swear that the judge sounded exactly like Psycho Stu.

Dad also got involved at that point, and told Trumpshaw senior that technically his jet was breaking the rules, because it contained ACTUAL PARTS from a jet.

And so they DiSQUALiFiED him as well.

Nice one, Dad.

Anyway, it was our turn!

Mr Hammond and Dad lined us up on the pier.

I started to feel very nervous.

Superdog started to feel very nervous

Percy threw up over the side of the trolley . . .

And then before we knew it, we were rolling at
FULL SPEED down the pier.

That was until Dad slipped on a puddle, and then that tripped Mr Hammond too!

And sure enough, the awesome JET OF JUSTICE came to a halt right at the edge of the runway.

Typical.

I turned round to get Dad's attention, and I saw Mum running out of the cafe waving her arms around, holding up her wind speed meter and trying to shout something.

I could feel the wind picking up. **IN FACT**, I saw that Percy was desperately wrestling with his helmet just to keep it on his head!

Then, **OUT OF NOWHERE**, the jet of justice was lifted off of the pier and propelled over the water.

Yes, you heard right : **OVER THE WATER.**
WE WERE FLYING!!!

For about four seconds . . .

Then the wind **DROPPED**.

And we **DROPPED** pretty quickly too.

We had to grab onto the side of the trolley to stop ourselves from falling out!!

Superdog seemed to *levitate* for a moment, but then he dropped back into his pilot's seat once we had landed in the water.

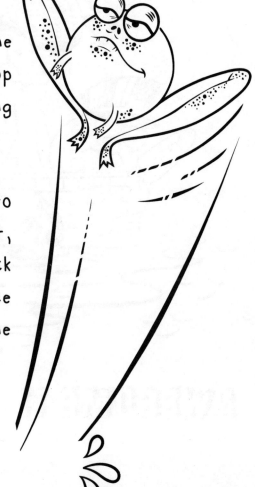

BUT, with all of the bubble wrap on the trolley, we drifted along the water quite nicely.

AWESOME !!

The lifeguard came out in his boat to pick us up.

And we INSISTED that he attach the
AWESOME JET OF JUSTICE
to the back to take it back to shore.

He said people usually just leave them behind, but there was no way I was going to abandon our jet after that **SPECTACULAR DISPLAY** of our genius abilities.

Dad was hopping around madly at the edge of the water when we arrived back.

Mum looked pretty horrified, and was shouting '**I TOLD YOU**' at Dad a lot.

Anyway, we weren't sure if we had won.

We couldn't be sure how far from the pier we had actually got.

Dad was hardly helping – he was too excited that the jet had even **TAKEN OFF** to tell us how far we'd gone.

Mr Hammond and Grandad Leonard were still on the pier, so we rushed back over to find over the results.

The lady got back on her podium, although this time she was wearing a long raincoat, a hat and there was a man stood next to her holding an umbrella over her head.

Lady: Well done everybody and thank you all for taking part! Although the weather has been – err – **AWFUL**, it has been a great event. So, let's announce this year's **WINNER** of that wonderful trip to Spain . . .

I looked at Superdog . . .

Superdog looked at Percy . . .

Percy looked at Mr Hammond, who looked at Grandad, who looked at Dad . . .

And then suddenly, Mum shouted . . .

Mum: Get on with it!

Lady: Well, err, yes. The winner is the

JET OF JUSTICE.

HURRAY!

We all cheered very loudly.

Although not loud enough to block out smug, full-of-himself, twit-faced Gareth Trumpshaw shout 'it's not fair!' **AGAIN**.

The lady came down from her podium (closely followed by the man carrying the umbrella) and handed us an envelope with our tickets.

AWESOME!

Now we could get to Spain just like **METAL FACE** wanted us too!!

I mean, I did feel some guilt. We only won because Mum's weather predictions came true.

But we did beat Gareth Trumpshaw and create a great invention worthy of **METAL FACE!!**

And Mum would be rewarded too with her ticket to Spain. I hoped she'd be distracted by this and not remember that back at home, the lawn was getting really long . . .

DANNY DINGLE presents . . .

YOUR VERY OWN SUPER-SECRET SPY NOTEBOOK!!

(TA-DA!!!!)

WOAH! What an adventure!

Now that I'm a **CHAMPiON**, I think I need to relax and have a little bit of fun! Genius brains need to unwind, you know.

In the next pages you're going to find some really **AWESOME** things to do, that I totally invented! (Percy might have helped a tiny bit.)

DESIGN A HOUSE FOR SUPERDOG!

Since Mum won't let Superdog in the house anymore. I think we need to design him a new home. Use your **GENIUS** brain and create something **AWESOME!**

MAKE YOUR VERY OWN JET OF JUSTICE!

If you want to be a champion like me, you're going to need an **AWESOME** way to travel! Luckily I'm sharing my secret plans for **THE JET OF JUSTICE**, so you can make your own!

First: Colour in your Jet on the opposite page Make sure it looks **REALLY** cool. Is it made out of metal? Will it have an **AWESOME** flame paint job?! Those are my ideas, but you can use them just this once if you like.

Secondly: Cut around the black lines! If you need any help, you should ask one of your parents or a teacher. See, they **CAN** be useful sometimes!

Thirdly: Glue all of the folds and stick the whole thing together. **EASY PEASY!**

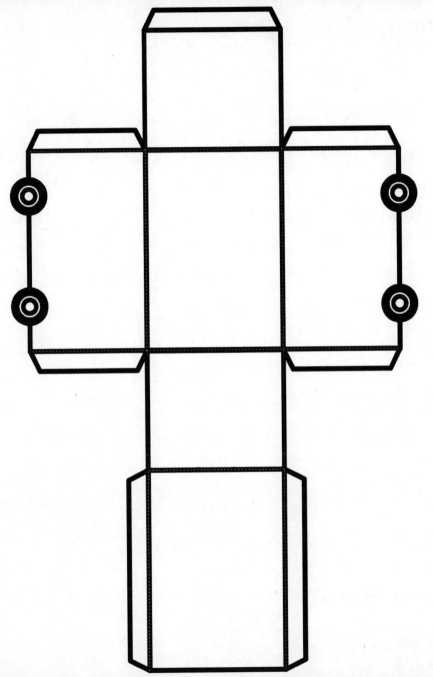

249

SUPER AWESOME EXTRAS

Since I'm being REALLY generous, here are some extra bits you can stick onto your JET OF JUSTICE to make it better than anything that twit face Gareth Trumpshaw could ever make!

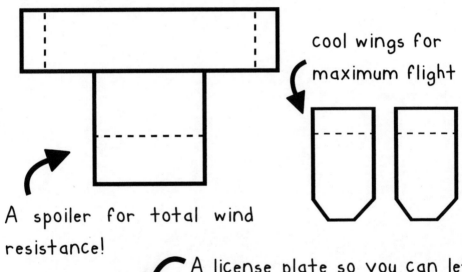

cool wings for maximum flight

A spoiler for total wind resistance!

A license plate so you can let EVERYONE know that you've designed the best JET OF JUSTICE ever! (Other than mine of course!)

PAPER BOWLING KIT

Percy and I LOVE bowling. It's just the best. Here are some bowling pins you can cut out and bash over with any small ball, or even a scrunched up piece paper. See how many strikes you can get!

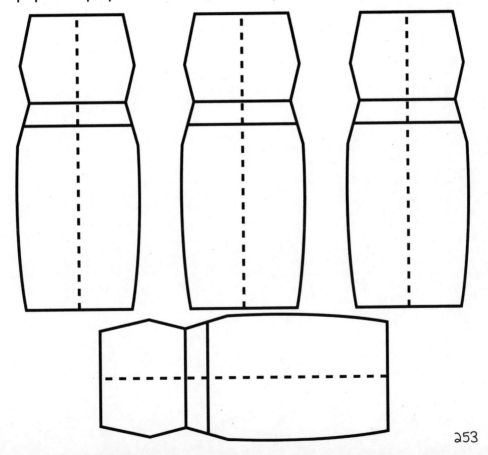

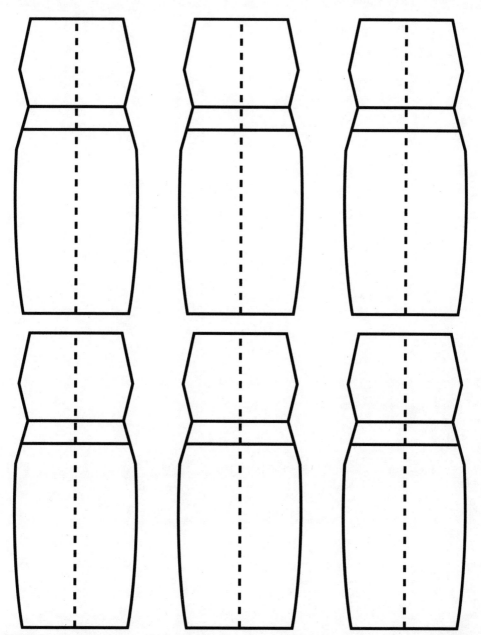